STECK-VAUGHN

PAIR-IT BOOKS

Family Time

Written by Jerald Halpern

STECK-VAUGHN
COMPANY

A Division of Harcourt Brace & Company

Families read.

Families teach.

Families clean.

Families cook.

Families talk.

Families play.

Families love!